TREMOLO

The National Poetry Series was established in 1978 to ensure the publication of five poetry books annually through participating publishers. Publication is funded by the late James A. Michener, the Copernicus Society of America, Edward J. Piszek, the Lannan Foundation, the National Endowment for the Arts, and the Tiny Tiger Foundation.

2000 Competition Winners

Jean Donnelly of Washington, D.C., *Anthem*
Chosen by Charles Bernstein, to be published by Sun & Moon Press

Susan Atefat Peckham of Michigan, *That Kind of Sleep*
Chosen by Victor Hernández Cruz, to be published by Coffee House Press

Spencer Short of Iowa, *Tremolo*
Chosen by Billy Collins, to be published by HarperCollins Publishers

Rebecca Wolff of New York, *Manderley*
Chosen by Robert Pinsky, to be published by University of Illinois Press

Susan Wood of Texas, *Asunder*
Chosen by Garrett Hongo, to be published by Viking Penguin

TREMOLO

P O E M S

Spencer Short

Perennial

An Imprint of HarperCollins*Publishers*

HarperCollins books may be purchased for educational, business, or sales promotional use. For information please write: Special Markets Department, HarperCollins Publishers Inc., 10 East 53rd Street, New York, NY 10022.

FIRST EDITION

Designed by Joseph Rutt

Library of Congress Cataloging-in-Publication Data

Short, Spencer.
    Tremolo : poems / by Spencer Short. — 1st ed.
    p. cm
    ISBN 0-06-093568-5
      I. Title

PS3619.H67 T74 2001
811'.6—dc21

                                                        2001024093

01 02 03 04 05 ❖/RRD 10 9 8 7 6 5 4 3 2 1

For my brother

Contents

Der Neuen Gedichte

One enters as one enters
the greathouse, each to himself
a carnival of regret & a hundred acres.
Each to himself a hundred tremors & an aleph
to X their epicenter;
to each a pile of dirt; a Letter: My dear fuckers,
I've had enough & off to the Hotel DMZ
& laid upon the crisp sheets of the never-happened.
Our child October's gone renal in yellow & red,
autumn's diadem: Around here, my dears, no one sleeps.

TREMOLO

I Am Cinematographer

A.

Clouds rally like cattle along the horizon.
From my window I can see the entire apparatus: the wheels,
the levers & wires. The pulleys.
Angels sleep in the luminous bedclothes of those
of us who believe in angels. Skinny, hairless, I resemble the fallen
child stars of each of my different youths.
Like Schoenberg's unplayable String Trio
my heart is reinventing the aesthetic.

B.

My heart is as large as a small mid-western city.
The city is soaking in a glass of water.
It springs open before me like a lock on a box.
It is the lock & it is the box.
It is full of narrow cobblestone streets.
I am a cinematographer. The pulleys. The wires.
From my window I can see the entire apparatus.
One of my legs is not like the other.
It throws everything off.

There Is Nothing to Not Be Amazed At

There's me screaming at my student
on the porch, bourbon staining my good white shirt,
the yard percolating with crickets.
To say the world is not shot through with loss
is a form of foolishness. To say it is,
melodrama. Yes X, the mind drifts north
but only for a moment. There's me,
age 7, smiling in my floppy hat, & there's me,
again, it's Sunday, & I'm driving her
through the corded throat of the Big Apple,
the traffic a clusterfuck & my alignment's gone wiggy.
It's more a question of how than who. More a question
of what than when. Understand? And then
I'm back among the shepherded trailers
of Sentman Dist., schlepping kegs, the sun
glistening pastoral on their still-wet silver shells.
So much unravels like faith itself, like the narrative itself,
I don't know what to make of it, it's just so many
X's & O's, just so many audibles rising mutely
into the sold-out stands. Who knows
what to say? When I have children I'll say
Children, eat your mutton, eat your peas. I'll say
Publish early, publish often. I'll seal them
into bed head to toe; I'll ask
Have you said your pantoums? Have you prayed
to the benevolent spirit of the reversed first foot?
This version of my life I'll call New Formalism or
"How a Meadow Saved My Soul."
The contemporary garden, I've read, establishes

a false sense of stability all the while serving as
antithesis to the reality outside its frame.
Okay, but what I can't
understand is how one moment you're
having eggs in the Village, drinking coffee that tastes
like static, cholesterol racing along the arterial track,
you're thinking This is it,
this is my life, it's finally happening to me
& in Technicolor, too, on the big screen, no more
straight-to-video for this starlet! & the next
there's that inexorable dust jamming
your pencils. You've got to
snake slime from your pipes. You've got
an audit & shit to show for receipts. I'm talking
quiet desperation here. I'm talking
desolation. I'm talking about
M jerking off to East Asian coprophilia
in the cybernetic light of 3 a.m., talking about
the sound of the dune buggy crushing poor Francis
against its forehead like a can.
What strange algebra all of this seems, now.
The drunken, hot-rodding kids. The drunken poet.
The waves slowly erasing the shore with
their tiny, salty hands. It's enough
to drive you batfuck, C.D. said, talking about
metaphors I think. I'm batfuck for X,
it's only been three days, & she's got a boyfriend.
Try & convince me the world's not full
of possibility. I'm Spencer. I'm three fingers gin,

one finger tonic. I'm one stiff drink.
Morning comes on like an ulcer.
It has nothing to do with stress. When
someone says Pay attention in the darkened
classroom, I've learned, you'd better hide
your knuckles, you'd better listen.

Romanticism

Fog heaved in like a headache only more ambitious.
The crane there. The wrecking ball with the one thought
it holds over all of our heads like

that moment in Whitman where it all breaks down,
ego/epic/subject/object, just that litany of
death death death death death wheeled out from
the storehouse of the subconscious,

nothing but the smallest strophic pebbles proffered
as offering along the windowsill. Which is one way of cheating
our tutelary gods. Part of me thinks kissing X in the park

among the belted trees another. The lashed & struck.
All of those diverging paths, Kenneth Koch's apartment towering
over us & no softball game to be found anywhere among
the bag lunches, the systolic thwack & scuffle

from the tennis courts. Our shaky administration
already suffering its final hours but what can you do?
The world's burning & lost in its burning.

Not even the ghost of a pulse, blue lips & yet
you go on pressing palm to chest, palm to chest, listening
for breath. Now the leaves enacting their strange vorticist twists.
Now the buildings with their semaphore of light.

How poetic to be young & losing one's love
in New York autumn though not the hangover.
Not the long drive home through the numinous tollbooths

& toxic correlative of industrial New Jersey. Subject,
object, ego. The cruelty with which the industrious, necessary
little ants of our despair burn so crisply beneath
the Romantic magnifying glass of language,

a little carbon-smudge of nothing where
once there was firm exoskeleton, a stern work ethic.
Though Keats might disagree & who am I to argue

with John Keats? 1795–1821. Of the bloody pillow.
Death & Eros. Part doomed genius, part sickly little brother.
Sometimes I think my worry violates all jurisdiction
as when imagining her going to fetch

something Classical from her car amid the multilingual
skitter & scree of 2 a.m. I feel a panic in my knees like
just before the crash. Other times it's enough

just to read Keats's letters, drink a beer,
watch the yard slip quietly into its petticoat of darkness:
how in the one to his brother the soul emerges only
after great effort & even then along a steady

dialectic of loss & more loss, each of us
perambulating our own dim forest of predatory grandmothers
& invidious wolves, our bread crumbs eaten hours ago

in a moment of now-embarrassing weakness.
Which explains, I think, the kiss. Her in the restaurant yelling.
To fully understand this, first you must write the paper
entitled: "Dialectics of Naivete & Nostalgia:

The Birth of the Soul in Whitman & Keats" which
will be presented at one, at three, & after the buffet. First you must
negotiate the Cliffs of Low-Spirits with sails tattered

& ablaze. Reduce. Reuse. Recycle. Certain ideas
should be avoided: the surprise visit after months of
not talking, clematis in hand or no. The spontaneous
proposal of marriage or its corollary,

the sudden desire to disrupt a marriage by (a) bomb threats,
or (b) the banging of fists on church windows. Either of which
may be found in some combination with (c) the hysterical

screaming of your intended's name into a vast &
seedless night. There are many forms of love. Of which,
these are not the best. I love you as a sheriff searches for a walnut
writes Kenneth Koch in "To You" & though I don't know

who he's talking about I believe him like I believe
the walnut is the key to a crime in which we've all been implicated.
It's terrible sometimes, this completion through subtraction.

The eddies, the wreckage, the things remembered.
The glints & glimpses. On the street, the smell of souvlaki
mixing with the rain. And in the park, wet grass,
mist rising from the mouths of small dogs.

As One, Creaking, Carries His Enormous Head Through the Bazaar, So Each of Us Is Carried Through the Bizarre

Something is falling: it may be a satellite,
it may be the temperature. It may be *the light falling*
lightly among the rushes as I walked last fall
along the river's pitch though
the river's just a rhetoric & full of
the wasp-like winding of cars & *the rushes*
just a busy-ness, a business, by
which I mean the way "something is falling"
steps in as apology for loss:
because desire unfolds its map/ an accordion
in a cage/ because it builds an empty/
architecture in the brain;
because a "day," a "road," a "river"
may any moment now flake off into meaning
& an evangelical fire I love at night
the dream I am dying,
love at night the dream *I am*
dying like a shadow in a corner,
singing like a wasp in a jar:

Poem #27 or "Its design is like a forest & a forest is no design at all"

How can I paint its portrait if
it won't hold still? & who here *isn't*
operating under the "vague influence
of distant stars" or, at least,
medication? The day in rhexis,
ruptured, raining forth its bright
coins & great good fortune,
the vendors have laid the sidewalk
to waste, the marketplace tilts
its head toward the sun.
If there's a chthonic grinding
you hear rising from the middle
distance . . . "If there's a kite in a tree,
that's me" coos the poet-gone-
homuncular, mediocrity's co-pilot,
he's bowing, he's blowing tiny star-
shaped kisses to the crowd.
But what to do about X,
whose thoughts this very minute
are ranging far downtown,
they're wandering off
conspicuous as consumers,
in sandals & silly hats?
They're spending other people's money.
What to say about the sky gone
southwestern blue & so cambric-like
it's lyrically ripe with Eros & wishful
thinking, easy to love, hard to please,

the heart winding down like
a parking meter, flawless blank verse,
the body opening like a daybook.
It cleans & recedes the sky,
vaults majestically over
even Johnson County Detention
where just now residents are rising
into *Baywatch* & their daily
deconstruction. They're
cheating each other mercilessly at spades.
What can one say? "Nothing happened
to us that doesn't happen to things &
to animals." It has a certain wherewithal.
It leaves an empty bed.

Four Meals a Day

•

As one buys before
the amalgamated & steel-gated
storefront of empty shelves (read:
Closed [Electronics] Forever)
a square red hat & wears it for
just one day—because one is
in love & believes love is
like a square red hat—

It turns out that it is—

• •

—& then finally we were forced
to realize how difficult & serious
everything had become: even
the azure pond of circling swans
decorating our park into
froth & cake must learn to stand
only for itself. As animal. Vegetable.
Ephemeral. As one bears oneself
from one ruinous, urinous alley
to another/ As one kicks away
the burning crutch . . . Finally
it just seemed too *easy* (anthro-
pomorphic flora blowing up
everywhere like a jihad,

the meadowgrass quivering like
pale hair on the idiot wrist
of my small-town love &
even said small-town unfolding
a dimestore mélange of
streetlamp & smoke effect);
there's a certain sinking feeling of
over-production.
Of déjà vu/ of *verdure*/ of video.
The heavy hand of Casting Central.
Even among friends at La Cabeza
del Zorro the Boy-Hero's
studied; steadfast; suffering; alone;
adrift on a smoky sea; he is
the tiny port of St. Denis aloof
off the coast of the Malagasy Republic,
sans export, sans capital, a little World Third
& nowhere a cure.
Or else he is a silver candywrapper
tossed about a windy mercantilism.
Or he is a square red hat

• • •

—When will the torrential rains of
Rangoon end? When will the Weeping
Mother learn to turn & look upon
her Dog-Faced Son with love?
Intentions aside, it grows harder
& harder to tell *faith healer*
from *honest thief* because every-

one's cloaked in a caul of
shadow & ash. *It grows cold . . . it
grows cold . . .* I shall carry a condom
in my billfold. It's October
& in the seraphic vaults above
the angels stir, white as Caucasus,
tailgating in the crystalline autumn
ether as an epic rivalry renews:
*I'd like to take a quick T-O to Praise
the Lord for Instant Replay.* Yes. Of course.
& for the rain outside. It laminates the world
against corrosive effects

• • • •

—& later it turns out that it is
not. What began as a not unnatural
inclination to kiss a blushing
forehead is too soon returned sullied
somehow & thinly veiled, a little
Heuristic, a little like a Skylab. Because
a hat can be the right hat for one day
& one day only a boy grows
each day obliquely tall & stork-
like. At night he sleeps
the fey, folded sleep of a paper swan.
He is an orphan! He is a watertower.
Only he can see through the gauzy,
tree-line comb-over & into
the city's shy, bald heart . . .

Poem

                    Thusly I knelt
in the alley swabbed, aqueous, in taxilight.
Became naiflike. Under the 737 gone pornographic,
like a slug-wake of semen across the belly of the sky.
Acted as arbiter of THE WEEPING MOMENT,
a thin slip of wire affixed between two fiery poles,
horizon-song, a sign, a grey eye closing
its only eye to the world. Okay. A boy has lost his dog & so
said dog becomes free-floating,
a disloyal signifier amid an afternoon's quiet decompression.
For the first time Loss unfolds its beach chairs in said boy's mind.
Erects its forts too close to water. The sky is everywhere
gridlocked/Giant balloons salt the smoldering fields
of speculative fire. Thusly knelt I in the undone alley ashamed
& the taxilight was the music of my shame/Kissed her
on the curb thinking nothing desiring nothing.
For the first time Nothing unloosed a static weather in my mind.
Everything come running. Into. Everything bleeding into the other
until X: the blackbird eclipse or The Triumphant Return of the Self
for cash refund: easy to ask the Obvious Question: to solve
for X: to wear the big white coat: harder still

Poem

                    to determine if the falling
weather truly falls or rises in the kicked-up
commercial light of this Our now-sweetly
shaken globe of snow. Almost appalling,
the nostalgia playing sweetly [picked up]
The storefronts silk-screened in ice. Increatly.
Undone. By Ice. One enters. Determines
(see: *to deter;* see: *to mine*) the very
pulse of the moment: Do interest rates rise
or fall in the affixed nostalgic light
of our progressive market? Theremin-
waves of light on our stores & statuary
where figures fix Great Scenes of Lonely Enterprise
for the masses in the didactic light
(*syntax*) of our City Square. The cloud-glaze.
The Claude glass. White light on a once-white wall.
"I'm not the hero I could be/ but not
the dog I was" like *The rope hung between
Nothing & my neck* is a true sentence;
is a conduit/ is a joke/ is a gas:
Who here's not looking for clemency? The call
connecting *and & and* phoned in as afterthought
(see: *pardon;* see: *begging*) & the snow still pristine
for one glowing moment—caught pre-carnal; pre-tense

Poem

The blackbird eclipse reworked as beauty
mark. In the eye of the beholder. Must
be fully described/Must exhaust its own
significance: Thusly March licks a last
salt from its body & like a boy blown
on a bridge over the busy thruway
a new world opens redolent with? Fear?
If spring comes now will it ever again?
The boy is undone. Reworked as——.
On the thruway the colors of the cars
a cryptographer's dream but what are they saying
about us? A matchstick architecture,
March, gone up in sulphury smoke. Nothing
doing nothing done. Thinks only of *her*
& every thought is a thought undone by
its own thinking Is a Borderland of
Fading & Change: his body is a *car*/
His heart a *gas can* & he ashore
somewhere between. Because *bridge* is a bridge
& not a metaphor for metaphor
thus the boy is undone. Like injustice
(I swear) the story goes forever on via
smaller, more articulate forms. Like a glorywar
he suffers/ A power we once thought transitive.

Empiricism

Skeptic *par excellence*,
Hume, he assumed nothing, not even that something
cannot *be & not be*, thinking of language,
perhaps, or—because I'm sentimental—the small wounds
we leave each day with the careless edge of our mis-
directed love. Tangelos, fresh melon, this new version
of the old order, the old idea we mostly hurt
the ones we love, casting a primacy on proximity
even in this era of fiber-optics. Of ICBMs.
Of red-eyes for cheap to China.
By which I mean whatever it is that says
the woman who is all tasseled leather (we'll say
it's Tuesday night) & in town for the thirty-ninth annual
Great Lakes Pow Wow is hurling poolballs across
the billiards room of The 8-Ball Saloon
out of some steadfast fidelity
to their intended. Whatever it is
that says I slept with Y in her fern-riddled
studio apartment in Fells Point,
writhing away at Degree Zero, falling down,
drunk, the shower curtain still gripped in my hand,
because my love for X had left me hollow-hearted
& pie-eyed with wanderlust & envy.
How to explain the stitches to X?
How to explain the missing watch? The broken glasses?
This is the story of how I came to find myself unlovable
& then changed my mind. This is the story
of how I came to understand that
the ego (soul/spirit/self) is merely a chiaroscuro'd
inner-screen on which is played out the talk-show of

the body's history. There's a coldfront
looming to the southwest,
bunched together like a coast range of hills
against the horizon. Yesterday snow,
& tomorrow snow, & today, too,
on TV, the cars have run down like toys
on the interstate, nosing the soft, white drifts.
It's April & although the ice wields its giant eraser,
still the nouns & verbs spill forth,
full of weak implicature.

This Cold Gossip Is the Wind

settling into the trees like prayer
into a pilgrim. Things seem to clear up
for a moment & then suddenly they're blurred—
a fog-shrouded road through the steep pine,
or the KIKE someone wrote in chalk on the sidewalk
in front of Andy's apartment, which lasted for
two weeks until finally it rained. And then
suddenly they're lost, wandering
the streets in their yellow windbreakers,
their vitals scattered across the milk cartons
of America. Before you know it they're just some hair
you've kept for years in a box beneath the bed.
I'm not going to be a slave to your pedant morality
one voice on TV is saying to another
while gripping the railing with one hand &
a martini in the other. *I'm not going to be some*
anodyne replacement for an abstract idea
X said to me, after walking out of the bar
& over the railroad tracks to the water, which we
listened to for a while. Which we listened to,
dwarfed by the tanker that was only
a black mass & a string of lights
consuming the river. How far we'd come
from the scorched earth & bunk trifecta of our
first dates: soppy kiss, fumbling grope for the breast,
then dive for the crotch. Enough, she said finally, enough.
Though that was later, on the porch,
listening to insects wind the night like a watch.
Sometimes what's absent defines the mood.
Painters of the Sung dynasty omitted the soles

of their subjects' shoes to imply endless trodding
through endless snowfall. Here, the last shocks of corn
have been orphaned out to evening.
The seasons reel. Often what at first seems like
only a few dots at the top of the mountain turns out
to be rows & rows of budding tea bushes.

Bull Market

Calvino's allegory of Cavalcanti's short leap
from the world of the dead (i.e., the graveyard)
into the world of the living (everything *not*
of the graveyard) is excellent if only
for bolstering the young artist against
an early, certain, lack of acceptance.
A little breeze reels through
the white curtains & suddenly
the entire room feels different, puffed
full of paprika. *Anyway,* Billy has said (we are
walking downtown) *it felt like continents*
drifting apart in some prehistoric dark.
The separation, he means.
Its prolonged aftermath of fossils
stranded across the wrong grassy field.
Someone's toothbrush in the other's bathroom,
someone's books culling dust on a distant,
more temperate coast. Here, Indian summer
drifts its net over 4th St. with a near
panoply of signification: accordion music
filters from the sidewalk cafés &c.
The color of the now-broad mid-morning
light is the color of parchment held up to a lamp
for the traces of letters it holds in its stock.
Tarkovsky's peasant house,
erected within the walls & mist of
a ruined cathedral, may well be a re-presentation
of intertextuality or a study of religious reversion
amid the chaos of modern Russia but
first & foremost it is an image

of great luminous quality. And if,
in the end, the image is like a dog catching
its own tail, asking *Where do we go from here?*
who cares? The door still opens on
pages & pages of leaves. Rust blooms across
the cars of the dispossessed. One explanation
sees the renaissance of 1920s-style ballparks
in Baltimore, Cleveland, & Colorado as
a simple reaction to the play of free-agency
& the indulging of a middle-class nostalgia
for more stable, Ike-ean times.
The Cineplex at Briarwood is aglow
on all six screens with natural disaster: tornadoes,
volcanoes; the radioactive flak & astral rubble
that nature hurls at us, constantly, from up
on high. Everything hurtling at lethal speeds.
Like my credit rating for instance.
Like the body through time.
Billy wants to send her a card for her birthday.
What the hell, I say, Billy, & why not?
It's October 2nd. It's a bull market.

The Bedbug Variations

What *definite* means to the dying mind,
for instance: the finite. The end. The *means*:
spent street whose loose grammar cajoles, redeems
each Tourettic tic, each idea of wind

invented for us in stainless steel, each wing
folding quietly its map. Achingly,
neither *here* nor *there*, the taken body
arcs/wends. The wan light (a pulse, a wave) can't find

us beneath the grey gun of November.
The minute tucked inside the minute trapped
like a city under smog, a doll-in-box.

Remember? Who'd want to. All disinterred
& all abandoned & all beneath the thunderclap
& there we were. Dehisce. Rehab. Detox.

From the empty cup a greater leisure.
From *the whip* a body made newly whole.
Brushstroke. *Canvas.* From the Nile: fetid Crow.
From above: the meadow's *green caesura.*

After the thaw but before the welter.
After the climax & awash in denouement.
Sheets exploded. White. Vespered. Noumenal.
After pain a fallow feeling settles.

And then? And then we smoke a cigarette.
M: I left here a *child* & I returned
child; I returned *a canopy of debt.*

And when Crow flew west the whole sky reset.
And when I was *the whip's slow wake* I burned
& burned. I was *vesper & testament.*

Corporeality aside, finally.
Random discharge & inessential whatnot,
Our bright idea to *write our way in*, or out . . .
What? Each day a coin buying passage: truly

Now a grey thread pulls from our grey factory,
Old factory, I mean really, *the smell*; how
For *the sweet sound of the blade in the wood* I
Swing the axe & for the pain in my chest the

Opiates, Ben, & then I "Lethe-wards slink" &c.
Nowhere more obvious than Here, the body
Now like the sea ruffles its white sleeves. Would I
Eschew the moral for a burning letter? or

Turn the world into my own private *lucre*?
Split the difference between sucker & succor?

It would be cruel & yet it would be kind.
It dresses itself in a string of light.
It dresses itself in string. Of "the light"
It could be said we failed to love each kind

Equally though our failures be a form
Of love & law & each a new lesson.
O love, the law (& each anew) lessens
Us & like a bell rung it finds its form

& spreads from the center of the city
Through dense fog. Like language it is empty
Though dense. Fog-like, language (is it empty?)
Spreads from what center?/Rises like a city,

Its origins long-razed, buried, & sleeping.
Fog dusts the empty bell-tower. Housekeeping.

Solipsis/ as in Breakfast Tuesday/ as in
Three dark birds unlocking the elm, the sound of;
Eglantine tones of radiant rose & mauve
Narrow morning's margins & one imagines

Not, *my reader, mein Freund,* that this version,
Our version, large with largess, writ from above,
Sine & sign, is, anyway, definitive;
Farrago & faraway (like history's

Own history/like narrative's cursory
Narrative) *three birds unlock the elm* & leave
Without a goodbye. O cipher & the sieve
Our Version, our story opens on story,

Radiates endlessly like a gyroscope;
Calls us like a Rorschach, dangles like a rope.

Arduous. Night atop its grey grey horse.
Night-bees gathering in the tremolo.
And shadow-branches. Black gum. Tupelo.
The globe of light. The grafted course

& sleep unseated like a satellite.
Inching in. Our dire *luna* hung aloft
(via lamphook & wire) & cast adrift
halos the TV tower & alights

briefly spectral: thus concludes this broadcast.
Hence anthem. Hence: wind-in-flag. We leave you
now with The World of Dew is the World of

Do Unto: unforeseen crises: ersatz
fruit: waxy light flooding the vestibule.
I saw a majesty unfurl: above.

And there we were: dehisced. Rehab-ed. Detoxed
& all abandoned & all beneath the thunderclap.
Remember? Who wants to lie disinterred
like a city under smog? Doll-in-box,

the minute tucked inside the minute trapped
us beneath the grey gun of November.
Arc & wend, the wan light (pulse? wave?) can't find
either *here* or *there*, the token body

folding quietly its map, achingly
invented for us in stainless steel: each wing,
each Tourettic tic, each idea of wind-

spent street whose loose grammar cajoles, redeems
for instance, the "finite": how the end demeans
what the "definite" means. *Is a dying mind.*

Undiscovered Genius of the Mississippi Delta

It begins with a name.
It begins with a name & some paint & vivid,
primitive brushstrokes. It begins with the 5 train,
which rattles its way from Lexington Ave. through the Bronx
3x a day, begins with anachronistic sloganeering
like The Whole Livery Line Who Bow Like This
With The Money All Crushed Down Into These Feet.
It begins with the flattening of Max Schmeling by Joe Louis
in New York in 1938 or Joe Frazier by Muhammad Ali
in the steamy jungle air of Manila, 1975.
It begins with the Beatles & it's all downhill from there,
my father's barber is prone to saying,
hair drifting down around his feet. It begins
with the flattening of time in the Foucauldian sense.
It begins with the name & large, empty canvases
supported by exposed wooden beams
& soon you've got a painting entitled *Zydeco* or one
called *Undiscovered Genius of the Mississippi Delta* which
is riddled with trademarks & deconstructed history
& the next thing you know it's Tuesday
& you're carving a path through
the rarefied air of Studio X. It begins in Haiti.
It begins with an ideogrammatic word-system of slurred
Romance languages & private symbols for royalty & ends
with some dried spittle at the crossroads of one lip
(upper) with the other (lower), with blood beating a pulse
in the ears; it ends, perhaps, with narcotics flaring
in the moth-eaten chambers of the human heart,
ends with chamber music & the arrangement

of orchids & wisteria & innumerable friends
& strangers. Perhaps it begins & ends
with a memory such as: you are 7 yrs. old
& running & there is high, wet grass
which has soaked your socks through the shoes &
in the background there is the rustling of some creek water
over stones. This is my memory though I believe its power
is transitive. It begins at age 7. It begins all your life.
It begins with blood, broken glass, a smattering of feathers.
It begins with pain & ends with itself.
It begins & begins.

Divine Hammer

The afterimage which is the image of God.
Or the stormfront the river follows like a fuse
so that any moment now we're expecting

its fallout to rearrange our landscape like a new metaphysics,
dampness, fungal acridity, the difference between
Plato's bed & the Ideal

is that Plato had to make his in the morning:
shiny shiny life we call shelf life writes D
& I think he means this one,

the cicadas keying up in their atonal pitch,
the trees murmuring something about the *dew point*,
something about *ground zero*,

the cicadas rending like a machine,
yes, but like a machine bent on its own destruction,
even my heart a machine bent on its own destruction,

(who doesn't love the sky torn open like a letter?)
who doesn't love the way we're driven
to bliss as if across a bridge

at dusk, gulls colliding like atoms
& separating in the orange strata over the light
& broken glass we call "the inlet,"

the light & broken glass we call
"the teleological truth," who doesn't love the way
even our bodies collide & separate,

separate & collide, which is
a play called *Eros* in which I'm an understudy,
the way X & I collided promising

always, always to separate,
the way we're driven to the impossible as if
to destruction, as if to distraction

It Will But Shake & Totter

Many poems have been written about the turgid sea.
For instance: the one about the man & his lover on the cliffs above
    the turgid sea.
It is the English Channel
& he is Matthew Arnold in 1851.
Across from him: "ignorant armies," "clashing by night."

The armies are not French.
They may be stars if what we've always thought of as stars
turned out to be the fading chalk of a fading language,
turned out to be nothing but the small sparks of rocks
being struck by chains in the corners of the sky.

Like a Russian novel the sea roils & cedes, roils & cedes.
Fish do their fish-like work among its atavistic depths.
Notice how the moonlight glisters like lacquer
between the crests & troughs, the smell of the brine,
the heavy, salt-stung air.

All night the moon rings & rings.
All night the wind searches the cliffs for a flag,
a kite, a woman's hat.

Love, I say, let us be true. Let us be.
The world is but a darkling plain. A hill of beans.
We are the few & we are the far between.

WorkStation

Look at the sign asway & tied taut across the rain-slicked street:
it says Welcome to Your Defenestration & it's in love with a hundred
girls including my waitress, whose moleskin pants go
    swit/sweat/sweet
beneath Viconian fans as she passes by, ablaze, in black, run asunder
& besieged. What tender brutality is The Tidewater Grill! Meaning
    this is not the Crazy
Swede, the American Legion, or even the Empty Bottle where
    winnowed, widowed Betty
hovers behind the thermoset bar, positively hydroponic, a Love
    Canal, an apostasy
in an age of risk-free living; shape anomalous as if divinely built—
    her body—
top-down, out of bad wood, & lazier & lazier. The Blind Pig. The 8-
    Ball. The 702.
I know them all. I could go on. The moon drifts, a pink egg in a big
    jar
& the river runs as always into metaphor beneath the rusted railway
    bridge unused
except as canvas: Shawna I Love You Still, for instance: heart's
    carina, Krylon avatar
& purely, desperately, dialectic. "Eek" pronounced Old English
    "ache." The time's past to be amused
by such ritual transgression. The limned. The liminal. Once
    abreast we hoped
the results would vary, verily, one postulate succeeding another on
    the long drift down to gnostic
truth; postulate castling postulate, an endless cascade. A slippery
    slope

along which even the Empty Bottle might be returned to us,
  charged, in the neon light; the body prosodic,
synecdochic, the body *heartbeat*, the body *iamb*; wherein even an
  empty bottle could be returned for change
& all the change be put to use: the boats an alphabet
on the water, the water a centrifuge in the reeds, A estranged
from B a railway bridge of paratactic glee, part parhelion, part
  parapet,
a wind-shear of stutter held together by sheer force of will—
Look at the town photographed bird's-eye & time-lapse to reveal a
  nerve-like network.
What's the language? The rpm? The waiters are salt in the
  restaurant's solution. The clouds counsel
& come up only with "weather," variations on: structure fugal,
  involuted, a bit baroque—

"And I Have Mastered the Speed & Strength Which Is the Armor of the World"

And so.
Someone has written Fuck You in empty beer cans
across my neighbor's lawn. It turns out it was my neighbor.
They glow like little teeth. Someone has written

& written & written.
Someone subtracts my father from my mother,
discovers I am the solution, discovers solution is, in fact,
the wrong word. I am what is "left over"

you say & the wires dangle
like a participle over the streets. "I love you"
you say & the night goes off like a gun in a car

Story

Lloyd shoots pool like he's standing
in a puddle being prodded with live wires.
All spasms & twitches. In Geneva, no,
in a movie, in sepia tones & subtitles,
a man & woman in Geneva share
a small glass of pear brandy.
Someone else has lost her dog.
And here, where the red lights are
cast down like eyes, demurely,
like a face blushing,
Laughing Boy is chuckling to himself
in the corner or staring at the jukebox,
a tiny web of saliva in his beard.
There are intimate questions
assailing the world like tiny pebbles
of hail. Someone whispers I love you
in a dark room but he might as well
be shouting More light! in 19th-
century Weimar or asking
his cabby where the ducks in the park
go in winter. One moment X
is standing there in a grey scarf,
backlit by the window,
the next she's in Colorado dyeing
t-shirts at minimum wage.
What I'm trying to say is, after
she left, everything I did was like
wading through hip-deep water,
learning to love everyone & no one

in particular. Things change so quickly.
For instance: you are walking to work.
The sun seems unusually bright
off of the tall office windows.
You are wearing a thick wool sweater
& still the cold stings your ears, wraps its
hands around your neck. Later, sitting
at your desk, you look up, it's mid-afternoon,
you're sweating. Outside, the sound of
a landscaper's shovel could be the first bite
into a good apple. And then it's spring.
But this is not spring. The entire town smells
like dog food. The day seems so sad.
It can't even heft its own weight.
There's work to do today, it says, but why?

Caponical Throne

I'll take nothing back.
Not the high-proof flailing at the gates of dawn,
bodies clicking like dice, not the grinding gears,
the smoke, the blue door. One need only stand in the aisle
marked Produce to understand how the wan light
obscuring the bruised fruit makes all
of our decisions more difficult.
One need only press one's lips against
the cold glass to understand the limits of desire.
A word is a word & so one chooses action,
often foolishly. One chooses action often foolishly
& yet who can deny the bright moment suspended,
tensile, struck like a match, as just before the kiss
the boats on the canal are set adrift
like the hats of the drowned?
Hoy es siempre & still the enormous stone
rolls back revealing what? Still one wakes after glutinous sex
to a moment no longer tensile, to the short walk home
through the park where the trees that last night
seemed nearly epic seem now thinned
beyond belief. One may grow older & not wiser,
learn to dress in the uniform of respectability
yet always carry in one's pocket an emptiness
from childhood like a burnished coin.
Understand, just being empty doesn't make
you a vessel. Ice in rocks makes cracks bigger.
It's okay, I say. Really. I'm broken like a book.

Poem Beginning with a Line from Nietzsche

Around God everything becomes what? A world?
Is there nothing new under the sun? Is there *nothing* new?
Strapped down on winter's promontory; the sky whorled,

the word *sky*, the cord of it wrapped carefully, curled
like a word behind the ear, behind the eye, the grey-green blue.
Around God everything becomes a world.

Perhaps. Around seven the evening's pretty dress unfurls,
image of the tree in the field-of-the-image, season's acrostic,
    meaning's meaning,
                                its retinue,
strapped down re: winter's promontory. The sky whorled

uncontrollably for hours, the calligraphic elm, the updraft & purl.
JC: "If only for the fire in the brain's fold" or Is it true that
    everything is true
around God? Everything becomes what a world

should be & so is wrong. Recast, resold, retold, recalled.
The center cannot hold its signified, cannot hold its liquor,
                            takes a dim view;
strapped down on winter's promontory, the sky/world,

the metonymic "word" in abeyance, the crown of shadows in
    accrual.
Under the sun there is nothing if there is nothing new.
Around God everything becomes a world strapped down
for winter. From the promontory one says: & yet the sky whorls.

The New Math

Who am I to give advice but I say Yes,
Mr. O'Hara, live variously as possible, love no one,
take your vitamins. The life of the artist may be represented
allegorically by any number of stories: one departs Normal,
Illinois, only to wind up, days later, run down
like Nate, in a rented car, in Paradox,
New York. In all honesty,
the acknowledged delight of entering
Paradox is usually followed by the immediate exiting
thereof. Which is fine with me, the way it flashes
but only for an instant, like Barthes's idea of the image,
all stratospheric static & a crack of light,
that momentary glimpse of
the irrational. Days click by in a steady
numerical ascension not unlike that of the hand-
held devices used by guards in the art museums
of New York City. The smallest possible paradox
may be "we" if that *we* refers to Tanya & I wandering
the art museums of New York City
drunk & again at odds;
Tanya at work on a series of enormous snow globes
paradoxically depicting the horrors of inner-city life.
Perhaps the schizophrenic I.
One does what one must for the sake of art.
The difference between language before & after the Fall
is the difference in marriage before & after the affair,
is the difference between baseball & a movie
about baseball. If one doesn't
understand this then one is ignorant of baseball
or language or both. If one's apartment is too small for

the creation of art it may help to paint the walls
with scenes of the antebellum South
& call it "Tara," it may help to
sleep on the couches of friends, on the floors of strangers.
One should sleep with a different woman every night,
wake early to write cryptic poetry on her
kitchen cupboards & doors,
open the windows so that the cold morning
can lay its cold palm between her pale & freckled shoulders.
One should leave without a word.
One should always leave without a word unless
leaving without a word takes such effort that it becomes
a statement in & of itself. Don't be afraid to be
an asshole, an old friend once said to me.
This he learned from Paul Klee.
Don't be afraid to be an asshole or a saint
but understand that around a saint everyone grows
quiet & there is much coughing.
"Money is an object" writes Amy L. 1998.
Art too is an object which may or may not translate
into money which is why it is good to come
from money if one is looking to
"make a living" out of art.
If one desires simply "to be" an artist then
it is not known if money can truly help in the creation
of art though it is not known if it can truly hurt either.
Byron had money & then didn't & then did,
which seemed to work for him.
To be an artist is to live always in the wake
of the beautiful moment desiring entry into

the beautiful moment. In this it is like unrequited love.
Hegel would agree. For if love is requited who needs art?
Writing about anything is like walking on a cloud
because language is both a presence & an absence.
To do so successfully you must jump very quickly.
One must not be afraid to enter the city
at dawn even if it is a strange city
& the language a dialect
that slips like rare oil through the fingers.
The city is either a metaphor for history or
the city in which you were born.
What is sex but a metaphor?
The difference between sex & a metaphor
is the difference between playing a sport & watching it
from the stands. No matter how good the metaphor.
No matter how good the seats.
If one doesn't understand this one needs
to read more great literature. One needs to
make love in the park in the rain, in a strange apartment
in a strange city. One must understand that one
can never read enough.

"Swedes Don't Exist, Scandinavians in General Do Not Exist"

& it's the truth innit? Seasons agog w/
their slow dissociation, despair tamping its genera
on the rusty fire-escape & all night we
drift through the city as through
the corridors of expendable wealth—
what we thought from the bridge
was the river lacked a recognizable currency,
dark as fir, what we thought at first was the moon
turned out to be empty postcards from
a radiant new iconography—the news
reconfigured us like a haircut,
touched us like a *sense sublime*. Pshaw, pshaw
sluice the black cabs past the rain-soaked
carports & for 4 yrs. I lived only for the radio,
I slept just so. Each station is a frequency,
each frequency a prayer, an ether,
a finer tone. O Delores who sleeps just so,
arms crossed, a crux, sheets tossed:
I fear everything & am afraid of nothing.
The yard is electric. Mail the coupon today.

"& Who Were They to Love Me Thus?"

Then, of bird & string, a makeshift kite.
The diachronic pulse of the moment.
Then the moment recalled like old money.
"Recondite ends." Each bright ignominy
having undone the mutual torment
of loose ends, the bird at once seemed both right

& wrong. "The bird" is a metaphor. Right
now it flies freely & I am but a failed kite
in God's black wires. Blue star of torment.
A cold rain & the street for a moment
is plagued with questions. So much ignominy.
Each thing devalued like so much money

wasted, wastrel, like so little money
that must go so far: past Boston, say, right
on to Bangor. One must ignore many
Sites of Interest, each held aloft like a kite
on History's string. The annointed moment
& scene of The Cement Angel's torment,

for instance, though what we might call torment
was different then. A Confederate money.
Sure, valuable in its own brief moment
but then exposed as gesture, empty rite,
each thought like a check one is forced to kite
to survive an empty age. The ignominy—

if we choose to call it ignominy—
is how each age fails to steer + mentor

the next, no good guide to assembling "the kites"
for "the tikes," not one black-bearded yeoman
whose copious notes fire the faded shiplog. One writes
& hopes to catch the very pulse of the moment

&, in doing so, fails it. This "moment,"
what does it consist of? Ignominy?
Drum beats? Circles? Seasonal rites?
The self-inflicted torrent of torment?
A city raised. Its foundation: money.
Then: a tongue, a voice, rising like a red kite

from green fields, the moment's anagoge, & each like a kite
two-ended, taut, rite & right, as if torment
& ignominy were our true currency, our poor, brilliant money. . . .

Journal of My One Useful Year

One more shadow & blur
emerging from the shadow & blur.
I've been in town exactly

137 hours. The last
leaves flicker like a tattered flag
& then don't,

the flag just hangs
there like a wrinkled tie. Here,
the streets buckle beneath the awnings,

the women wear strange glasses
or wear no glasses at all. Here, the men
have names like "Bill" or "Petey."

Each day my grandfather grows
more dead though like a good soldier
he took the cancer

down with him. It's 7 a.m.
& X sleeps so peacefully she isn't
disturbed by the yardwork going on

inside my head, she is not
concerned with conspiracies being
hatched by the grass's green army.

Trees peel off in layers
becoming smaller & smaller trees.
Understand,

just because the points connect
doesn't mean they cohere. One builds
a building brick by brick.

Here the ladders go all the way up.

Thieves

Same old corrugation. Same old rot.
Most days I'd rather be a bull in the china shop
of my beloved's heart than suffer these demands.
Even the billboards disapproving, the stoplights urging
caution, all our particulars blown asunder
like tiny notes from the refrigerator door.
That which is hidden is not lost though
it may never be found again.
Lord knows, one minute I'm a drone
going about my drone-like tasks & then here
comes Cliff with his enormous bottle of rum.
And then here comes morning with its pants
around its ankles. The fog, I mean.
I'm forever slipping on my own ice. You're
just getting used to the cold & then here comes April
with its head in the clouds, with its head full of clouds,
with its hair in its eyes. Rickety gait we call a limp,
family asunder, all night the moon keening,
the clouds with their seven veils.
Or not. Even God knew
to write in pencil. The body is tremulous
like the pounding of Brazilian drums in which opens
a yearning like the distance between waves.
Like looking out at a waste & empty sea in Cape Cod autumn
though sometimes even a parking lot will suffice: the "sun
    comprehending
glass," the wind articulating my beloved's hair. But who are you?
Gliding along on your bicycle wrought purely
of desire. One theory suggests time
is endlessly recurring meaning

part of me will forever stand, slack-jawed, amid
the sun-scrubbed grass, in my hands a quiver of weeds.
My heart a sidewalk natty with weeds.
In the lithographs of Käthe Kollwitz the end
begets an empty rapture though not in the poems of Keats.
Immortal bird! writes Keats though he means its song.
O succulent death! Light divides & divides
on the long slope down & in this
may resemble ontology.
Even our language a network of glances.
A room without windows. In North Carolina
Travis is surfacing in detox as if from the cold water
of a lake. I'm picturing him in the cathodic
light. There is no outside.

Ark Conditions

The endless pagination of days.
Days with their mouths left gaping,
days that sit in front of the TV for hours.
There was a time in my life I rode the bus
to work faithfully. The Hopper-esque,
laundromat quality of the light. Conversations
rattling like so much loose change in the pocket.
Ceeko said being in a Hopper must mean your life
is in the toilet, all that solitude & blanched
desperation. What did I know?
I was just another faithful disciple of Ann Arbor
Public Transportation, drifting through
the city like it was someone else's scrapbook
of buildings, people, places of benign to
negligible interest: the bus driver shouting
God damned knob doesn't know to go when
the light is green may be one version
of existential angst. The two women enjoying
risotto in the museum restaurant are, perhaps,
another: The first, having gazed at room
after room of Rothko's color fields (red on black,
orange on red, &c.) might be thinking about
the grey-silver mist that lilted from the well-stocked
fisheries near the house of her childhood.
As if a childhood could be housed. The other,
whose hair is pulled back tightly around
a pencil, might be wondering if she has
showered enough, or correctly, if she has on
Tuesday's underwear, if the iron is on & her house
in flames. It's a post-modern, post-Romantic,

Post-It kind of world. The flat glass
faces of buildings. The flat face in
the painting of the homuncular man, screaming,
amid bright swirling colors, from the bridge.
From Fordism to flexible accumulation.
Prominent scholars argue the most important
trend in contemporary architecture is not
the concealment of older, more beautiful buildings
by scaffolding but the impromptu cities
of the homeless sprouting like cardboard hedgerows
along the streets of greater Los Angeles. When X
ran her hand along the scoliotic question mark
of my spine I felt like I was a lock she was trying to pick.
That my ribs might suddenly spring open.
Instead I was a pig who needed a lock.
Igpay ocklay, I say. Beneath our common sense
ideas about space & time (read sexuality, identity)
lie hidden terrains of ambiguity, contradiction,
& struggle. X leaves for Seattle (my clothes
disseminated throughout the house in a simulacrum
of loss, as if the epicenter of whatever exploded
between us resided in my sweaters, my chinos);
I struggle. Pasta, because it is high in carbohydrates
& easy to prepare, is a healthy decision I make four
to six times per week. How I love the smell of fresh basil.
Steam rising from the brainpan of noodles. Often,
when the brightest stars are only pinpricks in a black box,
I throw a leash on the dog & go for a walk.

"What Seas What Shores What Granite Islands Toward My Timbers Come"

Corset & chord. What simmers quietly
all afternoon separating x from y; the moment's mild aporia;

the push & pull & I'm a caulk. A caul. Phylacteried
& the streets rupture outward like a corset/ like our bright flora/

like a rupture (x=x & is "a meaning factory").
Grey smoke. Market proliferation here. The forest

is a shipyard, mast-wise, & Osip, the shipyard rocks inviolately
under its cotton vault; its bodice-heart a fury of:

flutter. Aperture. See: I'm poking & prodding with my seeing-stick.
To left: things. To right: other things. Difficulty ahead.
I'm reading The Celtic Moon Sign Kit. Next up: Rituals For
    Sacred Living

(Chapter One: Unmixed Attention) & so the shipyard rocks aglow
    beneath
                              a floriferous fire & frantic,
dusk's infernal racket, what's left to be deciphered
brought ceremoniously forth like fresh bread from the iron oven
    (though
                              briefly) "forgiving

everything that happened between us" & then not/ Like
one puts a penny in the vase to keep the tulips virile/ Ties a furious
    thread
around the finger. There is the one at the center of conversation
                              & the one always arriving

as the others leave (Coincidence?). The wane & wag. &: A man loads
                    crates called Fragile
onto a ship. He is happy to be a "vehicle of commerce." He is the
    term between
production & consumption & the harbor swells lymphatic. Around
    him. Or, around him
the merely dogmatic wanes & what is left is "work." We choose to
    love him for this.

He is the term between the work & the work between the terms.
    He is the facile
heart of the whole facility. It ruptures outward. From the hotel. Clean
white towels across the terraced common. Chapter Two: Prayer.
    Mountains
remaindered along the horizon. The catalpa tree. The roof. Grey
    vapors from a green fan. Forthwith

each thing shall find its value by internal logic, a pure
    mathematics, agile
& ancillary: Not the gaze that is the labor between the man & me,
    not the prayer,
                    the like, wrecked horizon & middle
                    ravine.

It goes on. A shadow. A *no one in particular*. I mean in the grey hem
that is the dusk of the dusk, the harbor, the veil, & the gulls
    throwing themselves
                    again & again toward its sheen &
                    surface

Green Vermont

What I loved best were the green chairs
basseted along the grey hem, dusk unmoored,
fled like a woodnymph into the forest of its own dissolution,

as a kind of counterweight to drift,
as a dialogue between the distant & not-too-distant,
each notch a new register, a bridge, so that,

yes, the anonymous, indirect distances yield,
the whole recasts itself, as an assumption whose collision
makes all things possible, dusk folded back like goldleaf,

folded back like *the pleasure in a trope*, a narrowing of terms
one searches as one searches the underbelly of ice; a polarity,
    perhaps,
or the feeling of being both inside the moment

& out, like a game one erects at the end of childhood
that finds its motion in waves, that finds its end at evening,
descending, rising,

an anapest, a music, or a musk.

Good Peter Henry

By then we had grown small with ambition
& wasted our days amusing our captors with plays.
We gave the plays names: "The Luminous Particular" &
"Gaudier-Brzeska." We courted the tragic.
We waited for the waterworks to begin & when
they didn't we grew frustrated.
We set fire to the linings of our workcoats.
We longed only to be delivered from this,
the increasingly baroque architecture of our folly.
Nothing means what it did ten minutes ago
though it will again & each morning
the sun sets about its defining task: separating
the golden wheat from the glistening chaff.
O to be pulled like radishes from this unyielding *terroir*!
we thought & staged meetings, established fronts,
we called ourselves "the Luminous Particular"
& filled the already smoky backrooms
of disreputable bars with the smoke
of our worst intentions.
Poolballs clicked like beads. Calculating.
When, walking home one night, drunk on
the very dregs of revolution & rhetoric, I caught—
in the polished bumper of an official's car—
my reflection, I stood up straighter.
I liked what I saw.
Moonlight laced the street's
black boot. Wires
hummed tersely in anticipation. And
on the day all of this was

to come to fruition?
It is the way of the world to ripen & rot.
Nothing. At night we sleep like tiny matches.
At night the rain skitters endlessly across
the thin tin roof of our dreams
so that they resemble nothing so much
as the luminous city of Portland,
its helmet of light arcing though the briny air,
home of robust coffees, august, malty beer,
& good Peter Henry.
Peter, where are you? asks the wind
& everywhere the stopsigns wave goodbye, goodbye.
Or hello! One must never assume I say.
Meaning flies from me like a hat in a headwind.
I am slow of words, slow of foot. I am
both circus & sarcophagus,
the unacknowledged legislation of the world.
Look closely: at how the trees divide & thin into a winter sky.
At how the sidewalks labor under ice. In this,
& in this only, do they resemble our ambition.
O we were wretched. But only wretchedness endures.

The Hotel Eden

The parrot in its bright paper feathers or the window
opening out on an ideogrammatic landscape or whether what
    hangs overhead
might be "the past," weather, a plastic yellow ball—

we wander a hall full of doors carrying a memory like a key,
we wander a hall full of mirrors thinking our body is a key,

thinking our body is a box made out of wood,
the mind an attic, thinking duality &c. as the day
spreads away from us like a woolen stain across the agricultural
    blueprint
                        of the Midwest,
over the salt-light of small towns, over the off-white City Hall
whose posture is a symbol for rational substance, planning &
law but whose lack of parking suggests . . . Meanwhile,
the parrot, the ball rolling forever overhead, the small vial hiding,
pharmacotherapeutic, in the closet;
                        meanwhile
our childhood of scraped knees & irrevocable loss adrift
on Utopia Parkway—we try to go back but it only seems the wheels
    go backward,
it's a trick of film, one illusion among many;

meanwhile the bird goes nowhere, is nothing but
a paper dream of the exotic in a dream made of wood
while outside the window

language grows fertile & there's rain & there's rain

Years of Age,

ball of yarn, lonely frigate;
each minute a day, each day a month,
you get the picture, you do the math;
the imagination like the clouds a fist on the horizon,
invented from the inside like a tree,
invented from the outside like "a tree"
is a paper boat adrift on an arbitrary system
of waves; meaning I'm open but not too open,
&c.; the novel beginning "He,
stranded across the heathery hills dappled
with rain" & "awaiting orders via the luminous château
where heels count casualties across the marble floor";
facial hair, its removal photographed in stages,
as in: "The Seduction of Marie,"
as in the poem that begins: My love is
like an ice cream truck/it rings its bell for you;
burns up on re-entry; "The Architecture of Fear,"
the agriculture of Peru; how the heart
resembles mostly a fist-knot of arteries,
how the heart is a fist, a harbor,
a bricolage; last seen toiling as an extra on the set
of *The Fugitive Kind* circa 1959, the sun aswelter,
the humidity a bitch, just to catch a glimpse
of angelic Joanne Woodward;
O asomatic years of age,
nothing can touch you because "there is
no outside," an amazing trick, you predict yourself,
your wings flap a little & a dust storm kicks up
in the attic of *l'histoire de la folie*; or not, I'm drunk
drinking gin from a mason jar,

putting the strophe back in catastrophe,
see: "black box," "black boot," "ich, du"; see:
dusk's blushing décolletage; the sentence beginning
"if one replaced hymen w/ marriage or crime";
the night beginning with women walking
outside the window; the "walkers" & the "distance walked";
O years of age, ball of wax,
the ice melts, the night drops trou;
sometimes it's enough

Noir

Welcome disgrace as a pleasant surprise,
writes Lao Tzu. Prize calamities as your own
body. I once kissed a woman with one eye, drunk,
New Year's Eve 1989, in the driveway by her car,
the night star-flecked & in its finest dress.
Shined shoes. The moon hung like a watch
from its pocket. There's a cross section of one
of the old redwoods they've chopped down.
Have you been here before?
God she was beautiful, shivering.
The traditional method of creating scars
is to paint the area to be scarred with non-flexible
collodion before any make-up is applied.
As for color, newer scars will, of course,
be more red. I felt an urgency which I knew
was electric by the way my hair stood up
when I took off my hat. It was clear as a dark
hand in front of my face, as tinged with sadness
as the sound of boat hulls rising and falling
like sleep against the pier. As visceral
as the water that rushed through my clothes
as I fell through the ice, age 9, of the creek
that curled like a silver hair behind
my grandparents' house.
It was all of that and less and more.
In practical terms, Sarrasine's adventure concerns
only two characters: Sarrasine and La Zambinella.
Poor souls, working out their confused binarism
in the back alleys of some French fiction.
But it's always the binary: Gog and Magog,

Abbott (1) and Costello (0). Increasingly,
the lovers present themselves to friends and
neighbors as traffickers in a cruel self-deception.
Have you been here before?
It's November 9 and I've been sleeping in
with American Movie Classics, though it could
be January 1, 1990, snowing either way. Hence,
a great tailor does little cutting. And yet? And yet,
there's X, standing by the car, I'm clinging to her
like a sock, the night charged with static.

Farewell to Ida

There was the noise of the allegory & the noise of the noise.
There was the ante of Heaven & the bracelet of snow. City in ruins,
city *en luz*. Think of the fig on the table & the dust
on the sill & the hair in the sink & the worm in the fig.
Five stars. Durable pockets. The cord that runs from
Hence to Nigh is a system of nerves against
the scrim of the sky: was there not,
all night, the damp, inviolate, sleep of a job well done?
O lay me on the anvil. The plantwater. The codex.
I too believe there is A Greater Sea. A Something Epic,
a something to be misplaced. Whose white scarf is
a synapse of wind & once predicted in the dregs of our tea:
Tick. Tick. The flies wind down slowly. They are testing the limits.
Slowly the flies wind down. They are testing the window.
Tick tick. I think it is a coda. I think they are the "grinding gears
of a Vast & Metaphysical watch." I think they are a code:
The worm in the fig-on-the-table once read as
the Unhappy End of the Affair. When
the corn-colored noonlight addresses the mirror,
dividing the dark opposing wall, the dark & capillaried wall,
it turns *the wall* against *the wall*. December. Large trucks
rattle the polefence, the scrub grass, the carriage house.
The shops in the village swell like a sail. The story.
The smoke under its tongue. The figure at work behind
the shadowy screen. The wind sharpens itself
on the tip of a branch. Finally: The cord, the codex, the coda.
Finally: the secret joy. The before the before.

Subjectivity

Take this woman, her eyes adrift
on some interstellar pool of consciousness not unlike
the giant one in Lem's *Solaris* that turns out to be its own organism
granting the unfortunate desires of the novel's cosmonauts.
She is waiting in line at the Rt. 40 McDonald's for her
children's McDinner. She wears it like a cowl—
this subjectivity—her face swallowed
almost whole, a crescent among clouds; & *that* man,
there, his hand absently tapping his watch,
he returns to us only to
gather supplies for further, deeper travel.
You remember vaguely X saying something
about you being impossible to love,
beneath clouds & a few stars,
for instance, only to have it nestle unnoticed
at the back of your neck, eating away at you until
you're left mumbling, confused, a shell of
your former self like those luckless insects hollowed out
by parasites that drove Tennyson
to *In Memoriam*. But
this dreaminess is only part of it. One theory
defines the psychopathic as that moment when
one over-riding subjectivity consumes
a lesser, defenseless other.
It's a Kantian playground. It's *Us* vs. *Them*
at the cellular level. In the case of the serial killer
Jeffrey Dahmer this consumption
is taken quite literally. An excellent illustration
of the psychopathic may also be found in Flannery O'Connor's
"A Good Man Is Hard to Find," in which

a felonious nihilism comes
into conflict with a dyspeptic Southern family,
though a strong argument can be made
for the story as primarily an allegory of the end
of the agrarian ideal at the hands of a new, amoral technocracy.
But this is hardly subjectivity as most of us would
recognize it, each of us rooting around
in our tattered gunny sack of desire & neuroses,
each of us waiting in the rain outside her apartment to see
who she's dating now. Each of us looking for
that little pocket of protection against
the steroidal blitz of disorder.
Take S., for example, poised amid
the tarry beerhaus shadow and smoke of Mugs Tavern,
Bedford Ave., Brooklyn, humiliated by the woman
he has traveled hours by bus to see,
because he never learned to "give it up"
—it meaning him*self*—;
to the team, in the snuff & stubble vernacular of
his high school soccer coach; to the fraternity,
in the beer-bated breath of the paddle-wielding brethren
of AlphBetaEtc., as he was bent over,
bare-assed, red-cheeked, AC/DC brokering its musk
of Aussie metal through the stale air of
that wood-paneled partyroom in Rockingham, Va.
Which is why, in the immortal words of Patsy Cline—
desperate to surface into stardom out of
the cultural morass of nearby Winchester, Va.—
he falls to pieces, the first-person version of which is,
as I speak, transforming the jukebox in the corner of the bar
into a tender cliché of romantic longing and nostalgia.
He wants to take it all back, now. Whole years.
He wants to reel it all back in. Afraid,

perhaps, that if whatever has passed between
the two of them up until this—albeit bleary, beery—moment
changes form it will never go back, will end up, somehow,
always, lesser; diminished in the way all things
are diminished, eroded, squandered,
spent. Like water evaporated
& returned to earth, a little taken off the top
for new cloud formation. Like water squeezed from
the washcloth he's been pressing to his head—he's 19 again—,
de-hydrated, flu-struck, missing his Latin exam,
his legs too weak to reach the sink.
It may be over, it may be just beginning,
& I'm not sure which scares him more. His neighbors,
Margaret & Jimmy, the Penfolds, have stretched
their credit to its elastic apogee only to stock-pile
their three-bedroom Cape Cod with
the state-of-the-art in home security: their floors
ripped up & underlined with motion-detecting pads
so sensitive, Jimmy says (it's Wednesday now) from behind
the glistening avarice of his Toro WeedDemon,
Baryshnikov couldn't fucking tiptoe across them.
Their locks are encoded & double coded.
Their lights blink spasmodically when they're not home.
They're carving out their fortified niche in the world.
They're making the subject/object distinction.
And Nick, who inspects barbershops
& beauty parlors for a living,
who searches for health-code violations amid
millions of freshly shorn follicles, sweats off his last few
longnecks of Schlitz by taping fake wires to his first-floor windows
& sealing to his doors elaborate warnings
of high-tech defense. Imagine
spending so much money, so much time

(because time *is* money, because we *are* good capitalists)
to protect what you've already spent so much money on.
Imagine pulling out of your creditory tailspin only
to find your nose just inches above the ground.
What would Marx, looking up out of the moted dust of 1857,
from his research on German serfdom & landgrants,
in the reading room of the British Museum,
have to say about all of this?
You might be surprised.
In the oft-overlooked *Economic*
and Philosophical Manuscripts, 1844, for instance,
he bemoans the mortgaging of a visceral *now*
for a merely potential *later*. Go to the theatre, he writes,
drink more ale. And so S. might, now,
take a drink from *his* ale—
birthed just blocks away at a brewery resurrected
out of the abandoned husk of one of its prohibition-era
forefathers as proof that things can be reborn if not better,
then equal—as a celebration of that philosophy born
out of Victorian earnestness & born
into a world unprepared for its forceful idealism,
just as the iamb might be a beatific nod to the notion
of a metrical universe or the rhythm of the human heart.
Da-dum da-dum goes the human heart
& the poetry of Robert Frost.
But S. has a murmur.
Da-dum-duh da-dum-duh goes the heart of S.
Sometimes he wakes with trembling hands.
For a while in the story he is young
& wanders the boundless salt-flats of the female body
as if he believes angels might deign to descend &
guide him to some sacred book of answers hidden

amid its reedy wilderness.
They don't. He's not. For a while
in the story he is happy & then, suddenly,
the woman he loves is standing by the futon, weeping,
the toaster is bursting to pieces beside his head, stale crumbs
ticker-taping their way to the floor.
     Here's to Patsy Cline, because something
must always fall to pieces right in front of our faces
before we notice we're losing it,
& to urban design if only because it defines *prickly space*
as those architectural forms manipulated intentionally
to make residence difficult. Here's to
the uncomfortable wooden benches of the heart,
to those sprinklers we've stationed to douse
the dawdlers. One leaves & wanders the streets
in wet shoes beneath various illuminated billboards reading
Pinball Pete's & Dinersty: Chinese Eats. One hopes
that when the rock starts teetering back
Sisyphus knows to step aside.
One hopes. After all, what can any of us do,
rising to find the struck tree bifurcating perfectly our fortified den?
What can any of us do, in the end, about that third,
echoic, flutter of the heart?

UHF

Finally, the bullshit over.
Finally, the bullshit unbegun &
by bullshit I mean, you know, this.
I'm a leaky faucet, Forrest, a cog
in a wheel in a simple salad:
every 7 seconds someone hits Ctrl
+ Esc in my head & then ——. I'm a
simple machine: pulley, TV, shovel, hat,
paradigmatic lever poised between
certainties: nothing is certain is the lesson
with which the lever chalks the board. She is
& she is strict like the cruelest kind of justice:
my heart. My sweetness. My my. Happens over
& over again, the feeling something's begun &
will soon end badly. Spring, for instance; amethyst
in a glass dish; wisteria. Aerial recog-
nizance, helicopters lash Sky to salad,
little lettuce. Let us see clear to a loss of control
more proper, a seasonal patois, anima
of the senses, heliotropic bliss &c. It's old hat.
Tinctured. Tortured. I'm an aggressive robot. Caught between
nature/nurture & stature/suture. In each box a lesson,
disappointment: plastic spyglass, fake tattoo. Now he's
lost on the music-boat of youth, sighing *justice. —ice. Ice.* Ice.

Notes and Acknowledgments

The title "There Is Nothing to Not Be Amazed At" comes from Chavez's "The Unreal is Here." In "Poem #27," the quotations in lines 3–4 and 40–1 are adapted from Edward Snow's translation of Rainer Maria Rilke's "Childhood" and "Bowl of Roses," respectively (*New Poems, 1907*, North Point Press). "Poem" (2nd), lines 17–18, quotes Belly's "Now They'll Sleep." The phrase "Borderland of Fading & Change" in "Poem" (3rd) is adapted from T. S. Eliot's essay on John Donne in *Varieties of the Metaphysical* (Faber and Faber, 1926). Lines 27–30 in "Empiricism" are a translation from English to English of Terry Eagleton, *The Ideology of the Aesthetic*, p. 267 (Blackwell Publishers, 1990). The title "And I Have Mastered the Speed & Strength Which Is the Armor of the World" is from Frank O'Hara's "Poem" (*The Collected Poems of Frank O'Hara*, University of California Press, 1995). Line 12 of "Poem Beginning with a Line from Nietzsche" quotes Joshua Clover's poem "Unset" (*Madonna Anno Domini: Poems*, Louisiana State University Press, 1997). The title "Swedes Don't Exist . . ." is from John Berryman's "Dream Song #31" (*77 Dream Songs*, Farrar, Straus & Giroux, 1964). The phrase "From Fordism to flexible accumulation" and lines 46–49 of "Ark Conditions" are adapted from David Harvey's *The Condition of Postmodernity* (Blackwell Publishers, 1990). "It Will But Shake & Totter" was originally published in the *Iowa Journal of Cultural Studies*. "The Bedbug Variations" was originally published in *The Boston Review*.

Thank you to William and Donna Short for the support, the work ethic, the bust-your-ass earnestness. To Erin. To Riska and Walker for keeping me upright. To Ben Doyle for raising the bar. To Peter Henry and Tanya Larkin, for saving me at least once. To Wally "the Wine Guy" Plahutnik for the help large and small. To Mark Levine. To Amy L. and Cody P: what tolerance. To Susan and Mark Facknitz for the guidance, the opportunity, and the friendship. To Billy Collins for the obvious. To Jim Galvin, Jorie Graham, Simon Armitage, David Baker, Richard Tillinghast, and William Matthews. To Timothy Donnelly. To James Madison University, the University of Michigan, Andrea Beauchamp and the Hopwood Program, and the Writers' Workshop. And to the folks at Sentman Distributors, my other college.